THE SA....

BY

E. T. A. HOFFMAN

British Library Cataloguing-in-Publication Data
A catalogue record for this book is available from
the British Library

<u>Contents</u>

E. T. A. HOFFMAN

Ernst Theodor Wilhelm Hoffmann was born in Königsberg, East Prussia in 1776. His family were all jurists, and during his youth he was initially encouraged to pursue a career in law. However, in his late teens Hoffman became increasingly interested in literature and philosophy, and spent much of his time reading German classicists and attending lectures by, amongst others, Immanuel Kant.

In was in his twenties, upon moving with his uncle to Berlin, that Hoffman first began to promote himself as a composer, writing an operetta called *Die Maske* and entering a number of playwriting competitions. Hoffman struggled to establish himself anywhere for a while, flitting between a number of cities and dodging the attentions of Napoleon's occupying troops. In 1808, while living in Bamberg, he began his job as a theatre manager and a music critic, and Hoffman's break came a year later, with the publication of *Ritter Gluck*. The story centred on a man who meets, or thinks he has met, a long-dead composer, and played into the 'doppelgänger' theme – at that time very popular in literature. It was shortly after this that Hoffman began to use the pseudonym E. T. A. Hoffmann, declaring the 'A' to stand for 'Amadeus', as a tribute to the great composer, Mozart.

Over the next decade, while moving between Dresden, Leipzig and Berlin, Hoffman produced a great range of both literary and musical works. Probably Hoffman's most well-known story, produced in 1816, is 'The Nutcracker and the Mouse King', due to the fact that – some seventy-six years later - it inspired Tchaikovsky's ballet *The Nutcracker*. In the same vein, his story 'The Sandman' provided both the inspiration for Léo Delibes's ballet *Coppélia,* and the basis for a highly influential essay by Sigmund Freud, called 'The Uncanny'. (Indeed, Freud referred to Hoffman as the "unrivalled master of the uncanny in literature.")

Alcohol abuse and syphilis eventually took a great toll on Hoffman though, and – having spent the last year of his life paralysed – he died in Berlin in 1822, aged just 46. His legacy is a powerful one, however: He is seen as a pioneer of both Romanticism and fantasy literature, and his novella, *Mademoiselle de Scudéri: A Tale from the Times of Louis XIV* is often cited as the first ever detective story.

THE SANDMAN

by E. T. A. Hoffmann

Nathanael to Lothar

You must all be very worried because I haven't written for so long. I expect Mother is angry with me and Klara may imagine I am spending my time in riotous living and have entirely forgotten my lovely angel, whose image is so deeply imprinted in my heart. But it isn't like that; I think of you all every day and every hour, and my pretty Klärchen is ever-present to my inward eye, smiling radiantly as she always did. But how could I write to you in the distracted frame of mind that has been throwing all my thoughts into disorder? Horror has entered my life. Dark premonitions of an atrocious fate loom over me like the shadows of black clouds, impervious to every ray of sunshine. I shall tell you what has happened to me. I must tell you, I can see that; but the mere thought of it sets me laughing insanely. Oh, my dearest Lothar, how can I begin to make you feel that what befell me a few days ago is capable of reducing my life to ruins? If only you were here you could judge for yourself; but as it is, I'm sure you will think that I am mad and seeing ghosts. In a word, the frightful thing which happened to me, the mortal effects of which I am trying in vain to shake off, was merely that a few days ago, on 20 October at twelve o'clock noon, a barometer-seller came into my room and offered me his wares. I bought nothing and threatened to throw him down the stairs, whereupon he left of his own accord.

You will guess that only events from my own past that deeply affected my life could have made this incident seem important and the person of this unfortunate pedlar appear to be a threat. Such is, in fact, the case. I shall do all I can to get a grip on myself and tell you calmly about my early youth so that everything appears clearly and vividly to your lively mind. As I try to begin, I can hear you laugh and Klara say : "This is all childish nonsense!" Laugh, by all means, laugh as loud as you like. My hair is standing on end and I feel like imploring you to laugh me out of my terror. Here is my story.

Apart from the midday meal, my sisters and I saw little of our father. He must have been kept very busy by his work. After supper, which was served at seven in the old-fashioned way, we all, including Mother, used to go into Father's study and sit at a round table. Father used to smoke tobacco and drink a large glass of beer. He often used to tell us marvellous stories, getting so carried away that his pipe kept going out and I had to relight it for him by holding a piece of burning paper to it, in which I took great pleasure. There were other times, however, when he put picture books in our hands and sat mute and stiff in his armchair blowing out clouds of smoke, till we were all enveloped in a thick fog. On such evenings my mother was very dejected, and no sooner had the clock struck nine than she would say : "Now, children, off you go to bed. The Sandman is coming, I can hear him already."

At such times I really did hear someone clumping up the stairs with a rather heavy, slow step. "That must be the Sandman," I thought. One day this muffled clumping and bumping sounded particularly horrible. I asked my mother, as she led us away : "I say, Mama, who is this naughty Sandman who always drives us away from Papa? What does he look like?"

"There isn't any Sandman, my dear child," replied my mother. "When I say the Sandman is coming, it only means

4

you are sleepy and can't keep your eyes open, as though someone had thrown sand into them."

Mother's answer didn't satisfy me, because in my childish mind I was convinced that she was only denying the existence of the Sandman to save us from being frightened — after all, I could hear him coming up the stairs. Full of curiosity to know more about this Sandman and his connection with us children, I finally asked the old woman who looked after my youngest sister what kind of man the Sandman was. *— Something in German*

"Oh, Thanelchen," she replied, "don't you know that yet? He is a wicked man who comes to children when they won't go to bed and throws handfuls of sand in their eyes, so that they pop all bloody out of their heads; then he throws them into a sack and carries them to the half-moon as food for his children; the children sit there in a nest and have crooked beaks like owls with which they gobble up the eyes of human children who have been naughty."

A hideous picture of the cruel Sandman now formed within me; when he came clumping up the stairs in the evening I trembled with fear and horror. My mother could get nothing from me but the stammered, tearful cry : "The Sandman ! The Sandman !" Then I ran into my bedroom and was tormented all night long by visions of the atrocious Sandman.

A time came when I was old enough to know that the story of the Sandman and his children's nest in the half-moon told by my sister's nurse couldn't be entirely true; but the Sandman was still a frightful phantom to me, and I was seized with terror and horror when I heard him not merely mounting the stairs, but tearing the door of my father's room violently open and going in. He frequently stayed away for long periods; then he would come on several nights in succession. This went on for years, and I couldn't get used to the eerie spectre; my mental image of the cruel Sandman grew no paler. His dealings with my father began to exercise my imagination more and more. An insurmountable reluctance prevented me from asking my mother about it; but with the passing of the years the desire to probe the mystery myself, to see the fabulous Sandman with my own eyes, was born and continually grew. The Sandman had directed my interest towards the supernatural and fantastic, which so easily takes root in the mind of a child. I liked nothing better than to hear or read gruesome tales of hobgoblins, witches, Tom Thumbs, and the like; but over everything loomed the Sandman, of whom I kept drawing strange, repulsive pictures all over the place – on tables, cupboards, and walls – in charcoal and chalk.

When I was ten my mother moved me from the nursery into a little bedroom in the corridor close to my father's room. We still had to hurry away on the stroke of nine, when the footsteps of the unknown man echoed through the house. From my room I could hear him go into my father's, and it seemed to me that soon afterwards a thin, strange-smelling vapour spread through the house. As my curiosity about the Sandman grew, so did my courage. I often used to creep quickly out of my room into the corridor after my mother had passed; but I could never see anything, for the Sandman had always gone in through the door by the time I reached the spot from which he would have been visible. Finally, impelled by an irresistible urge, I resolved to hide inside my father's room and there lie in wait for the Sandman.

One evening I observed from my father's silence and my mother's dejection that the Sandman was coming. I therefore pretended to be very tired, left the room before nine o'clock, and hid in a corner close to the door. The front door grated; slow, heavy, creaking footsteps crossed the hall to the stairs. My mother hurried past me with my sisters. As quietly as I could, I opened the door of my father's room. He was sitting, as usual, silent and stiff with his back to the door; he didn't notice me; in an instant I was inside and hiding behind the curtain drawn across an open cupboard by the door, in which my father's clothes hung. Closer, ever closer creaked the footsteps; there was a strange coughing, scraping, and growling outside. My heart was pounding with fear and expectancy. There was a sharp step just outside the door; a violent blow on the latch; the door clattered open. Summoning all my courage, I peeped out. The Sandman was standing in the middle of my father's room, the bright light from the lamp full on his face. The Sandman, the terrible Sandman, was the old lawyer Coppelius, who often used to have lunch with us!

But the most hideous figure could not have inspired greater horror in me than this Coppelius. Picture to yourself a big, broad-shouldered man with a fat, shapeless head, earthy-yellow face, bushy grey eyebrows beneath which a pair of greenish cat's eyes flashed piercingly, and a large nose that curved down over the upper lip. The crooked mouth was often twisted in malicious laughter; at such moments two red patches appeared on his cheeks and a strange hissing sound came out through his clenched teeth. Coppelius always used to appear in an ash-grey coat of old-fashioned cut and a waistcoat and trousers to match, but accompanied by black stockings and shoes with small buckles set with ornamental stones. His little wig hardly reached beyond the crown of his head, his pomaded curls stood high over his big red ears, and a broad bag-wig stood out stiffly from the back of his neck, disclosing the silver buckle that joined his folded cravat. His whole appearance was odious and repulsive; but we children were repelled above all by his big, gnarled, hairy hands, which left us with a lasting aversion to anything they had touched. He noticed this, and thereafter he delighted in touching, under some pretext or other, any piece of cake or sweet fruit which our mother had slipped on to our plates, so that our eyes filled with tears, and disgust and loathing prevented us from enjoying the titbit put there for our enjoyment. It was the same when our father poured out a small glass of sweet. wine for us on feast days. Coppelius would quickly pass his hand over it or even bring the glass to his blue lips, and he laughed demoniacally at the low sobs that were the only expression we could give to our anger. He always called us the little beasts; when he was present we were not allowed to make a sound, and we execrated the hateful man who went out of his way to spoil our slightest pleasure. My mother seemed to detest him just as much as we did; for the moment he appeared her natural gaiety and lightheartedness gave way to dejected brooding. My father treated him like a superior being whose boorishness had to be endured and who must at all costs be humoured. He had only to drop a hint and his favourite dishes were cooked and rare wines served.

Seeing Coppelius now, the horrible conviction shot through me that he, and he alone, was the Sandman; but the Sandman was no longer the bogy of the nurse's tale, the monster who fetched children's eyes to feed his brood in the owl's nest in the half-moon; no, he was a horrible, spectral monster who spread grief and misery, temporal and eternal perdition wherever he set foot.

I was spellbound with horror. At the risk of being discovered and severely punished, as I clearly anticipated, I stayed where I was with my head stretched out through the curtains, watching. My father received Coppelius ceremoniously. "To work!" cried the latter in a hoarse, grating voice, throwing off his coat. My father gloomily removed his dressing-gown and both of them put on black overalls. I didn't see where they got them from. My father opened the folding-door of what I had always believed to be a cupboard, but which proved to be a dark recess housing a stove. Coppelius approached the stove and a blue flame flickered up. There were all sorts of strange utensils standing round. God above ! – as my old father now bent down to the fire he looked quite different. His gentle, honest features seemed to have been twisted into an ugly, repulsive grimace by some griping agony. He looked like Coppelius. The latter was wielding a pair of red-hot tongs and drawing masses of sparkling metal out of the thick smoke, which he then hammered industriously. It seemed to me that human faces were appearing on all sides, but without eyes – instead they had horrible, deep black cavities.

"Eyes, we must have eyes!" cried Coppelius in a deep, booming voice.

Overcome by uncontrollable horror, I screamed and fell out of my hiding-place on to the floor. Coppelius seized hold of me. "Little beast, little beast!" he screeched, grinding his teeth, dragged me to my feet and threw me on to the stove, so that the flame began to scorch my hair. "Now we have eyes," he whispered, "a fine pair of child's eyes." And he pulled glowing coal dust out of the fire with his bare hands and made as though to sprinkle it in my eyes.

At this my father raised his hands beseechingly and cried :

"Master, master, leave my Nathanael his eyes, leave him his eyes!"

Coppelius laughed shrilly and exclaimed : "All right, let the boy keep his eyes and weep his way through the world; but now we will carefully observe the mechanism of the hands and feet." With this, he gripped me so that my joints cracked, unscrewed my hands and feet and put them back on again, now in one place, now in another. "They're not right anywhere else! It's best the way they were! The Old Man knew what he was doing!" hissed Coppelius. But everything around me went black, a sudden convulsion ran through my nerves and bones – and I felt no more.

A warm, gentle breath passed across my face; I woke as though from death; my mother was bending over me. "Is the Sandman still there?" I stammered. "No, my dear child, he went long ago, he will do you no harm," said my mother, kissing and cuddling her darling whom she had now won back.

I don't want to bore you, my dearest Lothar. There is no point in my going into details, when so much must in any case remain unsaid. Suffice it to say that I had been caught eavesdropping and manhandled by Coppelius. Terror had put me into a high fever, from which I lay ill for many weeks. "Is the Sandman still there?" This was my first sentence spoken in health, the first sign of my recovery, my salvation.

There only remains for me to tell you of the most terrible moment in the years of my youth; then you will be convinced that my eyes do not deceive me when everything seems drained of colour, you will agree that a sombre destiny really has hung a murky veil over my life, a veil which I shall perhaps not tear apart until I die.

Nothing more was seen of Coppelius, he was said to have left the town.

One evening, about a year later, we were all sitting at the round table as we always used to. Father was very gay and was telling us all sorts of amusing tales about his youthful travels. Then suddenly, as the clock struck nine, we heard the front door creak on its hinges and slow, leaden footsteps stumped across the hall and up the stairs.

"It's Coppelius," said my mother, turning pale.

"Yes, it's Coppelius," repeated my father in a dull, broken voice.

The tears started from my mother's eyes. "But Father, Father," she cried, "must it be like this?"

"He is coming to see me for the last time," replied my father. "I promise you that. Now go, and take the children with you. Go to bed, all of you. Good night."

I felt as though I were being crushed between two heavy, cold masses of stone. I had difficulty in breathing. As I stood motionless, Mother took me by the arm. "Come, Nathanael, come along!" I let myself be dragged away. "Calm yourself, calm yourself, go to bed! Sleep, sleep!" my mother cried to me; but I was tortured by indescribable anxiety and couldn't close my eyes. The detestable, repulsive Coppelius stood before me with glittering eyes, laughing at me malevolently; in vain I tried to rid myself of this vision. It must have been around midnight when there was a terrible bang, like the firing of a gun. The detonation echoed through the whole house and the blast whistled past my room; doors throughout the house were slammed shut with a clatter.

"That's Coppelius!" I cried in horror, jumping out of bed.

Then the air was rent by a series of despairing wails and screams. I rushed to my father's room; the door was open, suffocating smoke billowed out at me; the servant girl screamed: "Oh, the master, oh, the master!" On the floor in front of the reeking stove, my father lay dead, his face burnt black and horribly contorted; my sisters were howling and whimpering around him and my mother lay unconscious beside him.

"Coppelius, abominable Satan, you have murdered my father!" I cried, then fell senseless to the ground.

Two days later, when he was put into his coffin, my father's features had become mild and gentle again, as they had been in life. I was consoled by the sudden conviction that his pact with the devilish Coppelius could not have thrust him into everlasting perdition.

The explosion had woken the neighbours; the incident was talked about and came to the ears of the authorities, who wished to proceed against Coppelius. But he had vanished from the town without a trace.

When I now tell you, my dearest friend, that the barometer-seller was the villainous Coppelius, you will not blame me for interpreting this apparition as heralding some terrible disaster. He was differently dressed, but Coppelius's face and figure are too deeply imprinted upon my mind for any mistake to be possible. Moreover, Coppelius has barely changed his name. I am told that he is passing himself off as a Piedmontese mechanic called Giuseppe Coppola.

I am resolved to have it out with him and to avenge my father's death, come what may.

Don't tell Mother anything about the arrival of the loathsome monster.

Give my love to my dear, sweet Klara. I shall write to her when I am in a calmer frame of mind.

Best wishes, etc., etc.

Klara to Nathanael

It is true that you haven't written for a long time, but nevertheless I believe that I am in your thoughts. You must have been thinking of me very vividly when you addressed your last letter to Lothar, because you wrote my name on the envelope instead of his. I joyfully opened the letter and didn't realize my mistake until I came to the words "Oh, my dearest Lothar". I ought to have stopped there and immediately given the letter to my brother. But even though in your childhood you used to tease me by saying that I was so calm and reflective that if the house were about to collapse and I saw a crease in the curtain, I should quickly smooth it out before fleeing the doomed building, nevertheless I need hardly assure you that the beginning of your letter distressed me profoundly. I could scarcely breathe, and everything swam before my eyes. "Oh, my beloved Nathanael," I thought, "what terrible thing can have entered your life? Are we perhaps to part and never see one another again?" The thought pierced my breast like a stab with a red-hot dagger. I read on and on. From your description Coppelius sounds horrible. I never knew before that your good old father died such a dreadful death. When I passed the letter on to its rightful owner my brother Lothar tried to pacify me, but he wasn't very successful. The baleful barometer-seller Giuseppe Coppola dogged my every step, and I am almost ashamed to confess that he succeeded in disturbing my normally sound and peaceful sleep with all kinds of fantastic dream images. But by next morning I saw everything differently. Don't be angry with me, my dearly beloved, if Lothar tells you that, in spite of your strange presentiment that Coppelius will do you some harm, I am still just as gay and light-hearted as ever.

I will admit straight out that in my opinion all the terrible things you speak of happened only within your own mind and that the outer world had very little part in them. Old Coppelius may well have been a repulsive character, but it was because he hated children that you children developed such an aversion towards him.

Of course the dreadful Sandman of the nurse's tale became linked in your child's mind with old Coppelius, whom, even when you no longer believed in the Sandman, you still regarded as a monster especially dangerous to children. The sinister nocturnal activities in which he had your father engaged were nothing but clandestine alchemistic experiments, which were bound to displease your mother because they are sure to have resulted in a great deal of money being wasted; moreover, as always happens in such cases, your father's mind must have become filled with the illusory desire to acquire higher wisdom and thereby diverted from his family. Your father's death was undoubtedly due to his own carelessness and not Coppelius's fault. Yesterday I asked the experienced apothecary who lives next door whether such instantly lethal explosions could occur during chemical experiments. He replied, "Most certainly," and went on to explain at length and in detail how this might happen, mentioning so many strange-sounding names that I can't remember any of them.

Now you will probably be annoyed with your Klara; you will say : "No ray of the mysterious forces that often clasp men in their invisible arms can penetrate that cold spirit; she sees only the colourful surface of life and rejoices over it, like the thoughtless child over the bright and shining fruit within which poison lurks."

Oh, my dearly beloved Nathanael, don't you believe that gay, light-hearted, care-free spirits may also sense the presence of dark powers within ourselves that are bent upon our destruction? But forgive me if, simple girl that I am, I try to show you what I really think about such inner conflicts. In the end, I shan't be able to find the right words and you will laugh not at what I say, but at the clumsy way in which I say it.

If there is a malignant power that treacherously introduces a thread into our hearts, by means of which it then drags us along a dangerous, a ruinous path which we should never have trodden of our own accord, then it must become part of us, part of our own self; for only thus shall we believe it and give it the freedom of action it needs in order to carry out its secret purpose. But if our minds are firm enough and sufficiently strengthened by a happy life always to recognize alien, hostile influences and to proceed with calm steps along the path chosen by our own inclinations, the sinister power perishes in the vain attempt to create the shape that is to serve as a reflection of ourselves.

"There can also be no doubt," adds Lothar to this, "that once we have surrendered ourselves to the dark physical power, it frequently draws inside us external figures thrown in our path by the world; then it is we ourselves who endow these figures with the life with which, in wild delusion, we credit them."

You see, my dearly beloved Nathanael, that my brother Lothar and I have discussed the question of malignant powers at length, and now that I have, not without difficulty, written down the main points in our argument it all seems very profound. I don't entirely understand Lothar's last words, I have only an inkling of what he means, and yet it all seems to me very true. Cast the horrible lawyer Coppelius and the barometer man Giuseppe Coppola entirely out of your mind, I beg of you. Be sure that these external figures cannot harm you; only your belief in their baneful power can make them baneful to you in reality. If the profound agitation of your mind was not apparent from every line of your letter, if your suffering did not cut me to the quick, I assure you I could laugh about the lawyer, Sandman, and barometer-seller Coppelius. Be cheerful, cheerful! I have made up my mind to come to you like a guardian angel, and, if he let me near him, to scare nasty old Coppola away with loud laughter. I am not in the very least afraid of him and his horrid hands; he isn't going to spoil my titbits as a lawyer nor my eyes as the Sandman ·

For ever, my best beloved Nathanael, etc., etc., etc.

Nathanael to Lothar

I'm very sorry that, as a result of my slip, Klara accidentally opened and read my recent letter to you. She wrote me a very profound and philosophical letter in reply, in which she sets out to prove that Coppelius and Coppola exist only within me and are phantoms of my own ego, which would instantly fall to dust if I recognized them as such. It is hard to believe that the mind which shines forth from her bright and smiling child's eyes, that are like a vision in a dream, is capable of such a sagacious and masterly interpretation. She quotes you. The two of you have been talking about me. You must have been lecturing her, teaching her to see and analyse things clearly. Stop it! Anyhow, it is now quite certain that the barometer-seller Giuseppe Coppola is not the old lawyer Coppelius. I am attending lectures by the new professor of physics, who, like the famous natural philosopher, is called Spallanzani and is of Italian origin. He has known Coppola for many years, and apart from this you can tell that Coppola really is a Piedmontese from his accent. Coppelius was a German, though, I suspect, not a true German. I am entirely reassured. You and Klara may continue to think me a gloomy dreamer, but I cannot get Coppelius's accursed face out of my mind. I'm glad he has left the city, as Spallanzani tells me.

This professor is an extraordinary fellow. A tubby little man with protruding cheek-bones, a slender nose, thick lips, and small piercing eyes. But if you look at an engraving of Cagliostro by Chodowiecki in some Berlin calendar it will give you a far more accurate idea of his appearance than any description of mine. That's what Spallanzani looks like. As I went up the stairs in his house the other day I noticed a narrow gap on one side of the curtain that is generally drawn across a particular glass door. I don't know myself how I came to do such a thing, but I inquisitively peeped through. There was a tall, very slim, beautifully proportioned, magnificently dressed woman sitting in the room at a small table, on which both arms were resting with folded hands. She was facing the door, so that I could see the whole of her angelically lovely face. She didn't seem to notice me, and there was a curiously fixed look in her eyes, almost as though they lacked the power of vision, as though she were asleep with her eyes open. It gave me an uncanny sensation and I quickly slipped away into the lecture-room, which is next door. Later I learnt that the figure I had seen was Spallanzani's daughter Olympia, whom for some strange reason he wickedly keeps shut up, never allowing anyone near her. Perhaps there is something the matter with her; perhaps she is a half-wit or something.

I don't know why I am writing you all this : I could have told you everything better and at greater length by word of mouth. The fact is, I am coming to stay with you for a fortnight. I must see my sweet angel, my Klara, again. That will blow away all the ill-humour which, I must admit, took possession of me after her terribly sensible letter. That's why I'm not writing to her as well today.

A thousand greetings, etc., etc.

Here I must add a word about the background to the extraordinary events which befell the student Nathanael, and which are introduced by the foregoing letters. Soon after his father died, Klara and Lothar, the children of a distant relative who had likewise died and left them orphans, were taken in by Nathanael's mother. Klara and Nathanael quickly conceived a passionate affection for one another, to which no one in the world had any objection to raise. They therefore became engaged when Nathanael left the town to pursue his studies at G——. His letters were written from G——, where he was attending lectures by the famous professor of physics, Spallanzani. ˌ

Klara was considered by many people cold, unfeeling, prosaic, because of her clarity of vision and impatience with hocus-pocus; but others, better able to distinguish the true from the false, dearly loved the spirited, sympathetic, and unsophisticated girl; none loved her so deeply as Nathanael, a man well versed in the arts and sciences. Klara was wholeheartedly devoted to her beloved, and the first shadow fell across her life the day he parted from her. With what delight she flew into his arms when now, as he had announced in his last letter to Lothar, he returned to his native town and entered his mother's room. As Nathanael had foreseen, the moment he saw Klara he thought neither of the lawyer Coppelius nor of Klara's over-sensible letter; all his ill humour vanished.

Yet Nathanael was quite right when he wrote to his friend Lothar that the entry of the repulsive barometer-seller Coppolo into his life had been fraught with disastrous consequences. This was evident to everyone in the first few days of his visit, for Nathanael's whole nature had changed. He sank into gloomy brooding and behaved in an extra- ordinary way quite unlike his normal self. Life seemed to have become for him nothing but dream and foreboding; he kept on saying that everyone who imagined himself free was really the plaything of dark and cruel powers; it was useless to rebel, we all had to bow humbly to our destiny. He went so far as to assert that it was foolish to suppose that man's creative activities in the fields of art and science were the outcome of free will, claiming that the inspiration which enables us to create does not come from within us, but is imposed upon us by some higher power outside ourselves.

The clear-headed Klara found all this mystical nonsense in the highest degree objectionable, but it seemed pointless to contradict. She said nothing until Nathanael stated that Coppelius was an evil spirit, as he had realized when he eavesdropped upon him from behind the curtain, and that this abominable demon would wreak havoc with their happiness. Then Klara replied very seriously : "Yes, Nathanael, you are right : Coppelius is an evil, malignant spirit; he can exercise the terrible powers of a demon incarnate; but only if you do not banish him from your mind. So long as you believe in him, he will exist and interfere with you; it is only your belief that gives him power."

Angered by Klara's refusal to credit the demon's existence outside his own mind, Nathanael was about to launch into a disquisition on the whole mystical doctrine of devils and sinister powers, when to his annoyance Klara brought the conversation to a close with some casual interruption. He thought to himself that people with cold, insensitive natures render themselves inaccessible to profound mysteries of this kind. But since he was not fully aware of numbering Klara among people of inferior sensibility, he continued his efforts to initiate her into these mysteries. While Klara was getting breakfast in the morning, he stood beside her, reading aloud from all sorts of mystical books, till Klara commented: "You know, you are the evil spirit that is threatening to spoil my coffee. If I were to drop everything, as you want me to, and look into your eyes while you read, the coffee would boil over and none of you would get any breakfast." Nathanael slammed the book shut and made off to his room, much put out.

In the ordinary way, he had a notable gift for making up delightful and amusing stories, to which Klara listened with the greatest pleasure; now his tales were gloomy, unintelligible, formless, and although Klara refrained from saying so to spare his feelings, he could feel how little she liked them. Klara found nothing more deadly than boredom, and her uncontrollable drowsiness was expressed in her eyes and voice. Nathanael's tales were indeed very tedious. His resentment at Klara's cold, prosaic mind increased; Klara could not overcome her dislike of Nathanael's dark, gloomy, dreary mysticism; and so the two of them drifted farther and farther apart without realizing it. Nathanael himself had to admit that the image of the atrocious Coppelius had paled within him, and it often cost him an effort to give life to this figure when he introduced him into his writings in the role of a sinister bogy-man. Eventually he made a poem out of his dark foreboding that Coppelius would destroy his happiness in love. He portrayed himself and Klara as bound in true love but plagued by a black hand that thrust itself between them and snatched away their joy. In the end, when they were already at the altar, the abominable Coppelius appeared and touched Klara's lovely eyes, which sprang into Nathanael's breast, searing him like blood-red sparks. Coppelius seized hold of him and flung him into a circle of flames that spun round and round with the speed and noise of a whirlwind and dragged him away. There was a roaring sound like a hurricane whipping up the waves of the sea so that they reared up in revolt like black giants with heads of white foam. But through this fierce roaring he heard Klara's voice : "Can't you see me? Coppelius has tricked you. Those weren't my eyes that burnt into your breast, they were red-hot drops of your own heart's blood. I still have my eyes – just look at me !" Nathanael thought : "That is Klara, I am hers for ever." Then it was as though this thought had taken a grip upon the circle of flame, which came to a stop, while the roaring sound died away in the black abyss. Nathanael gazed into Klara's eyes; but it was death that looked at him with Klara's friendly eyes.

While Nathanael was composing this poem he was very calm and serene; he worked and polished each line, and since he had assumed the yoke of metre he did not rest until the whole poem was flawless and euphonious. But when at last he had finished and read it aloud to himself, he was seized with horror and cried out : "Whose hideous voice is that?" Soon, however, the whole thing once more seemed nothing but a very successful poem, and he felt convinced that Klara's cold temperament would be set afire by it; though he had no very clear idea why Klara should be set afire or what purpose would be served by frightening her with these horrifying visions which predicted a terrible fate and the destruction of their love.

Nathanael and Klara were sitting in his mother's little guarden; Klara was very cheerful because during the three days he had spent writing the poem Nathanael had ceased bothering her with his dreams and premonitions. Instead he talked gaily of things that amused her, as in the past, which led Klara to remark: "Now I've really got you back entirely. You see how we have driven out old Coppelius?"

At this, Nathanael remembered that he was carrying in his pocket the poem he had intended to read aloud. He immediately pulled out the sheets of paper and started reading. Klara, expecting something boring as usual and making the best of the situation, quietly started knitting. But as the threatening cloud of the poem grew blacker and blacker, she let the stocking she was knitting sink down and gazed fixedly into Nathanael's eyes. The latter was carried away by his own poem; emotion had coloured his cheeks bright red; tears poured from his eyes. Finally, he came to a stop, gave a groan of utter exhaustion, took Klara's hand, and sighed as though dissolving in hopeless grief : "Oh – Klara – Klara !"

Klara pressed him tenderly to her bosom and said in a

low voice, but very slowly and gravely : "Nathanael, my dearly beloved Nathanael, throw the mad, senseless, insane fairy tale into the fire."

Thereupon, Nathanael sprang to his feet indignantly, pushed Klara away from him and cried : "You lifeless damned automaton!" Then he hurried away.

Deeply hurt, Klara wept bitterly and sobbed loudly : "He can never have loved me, since he doesn't understand me."

Lothar came into the arbour and made Klara tell him what had happened. He loved his sister with all his soul, and every word of her complaint fell into his heart like a spark, so that the hostility he had long felt for the visionary Nathanael flared up into furious rage. He ran to Nathanael and reproached him for his senseless behaviour towards his beloved sister in harsh words, which the irascible Nathanael answered in kind. "Crazy, addle-brained dreamer" was answered by "Miserable, dull-witted oaf". A duel was inevitable. They agreed to fight next morning outside the garden with sharpened rapiers, in accordance with the custom at the local university. They stalked about mute and scowling; Klara had heard the violent argument and saw the fencing master bring the rapiers after dusk. She guessed what was afoot.

Having arrived at the duelling ground and cast off their coats in grim silence, bloodthirsty battle-lust in their blazing eyes, Lothar and Nathanael were on the point of falling upon one another when Klara rushed out of the garden gate. Sobbing, she cried out : "You ferocious beasts! Strike me down before you set upon each other; for how can I go on living if my lover has murdered my brother, or my brother my lover?"

Lothar lowered his weapon and stared in silence at the ground; but in Nathanael's heart all the love he had felt for sweet Klara in the finest days of his youth came to life again accompanied by an agonizing nostalgia. The murderous weapon fell from his hand and he flung himself at

Klara's feet. "Can you ever forgive me, my one and only, my beloved Klara? Can you forgive me, my dearest brother Lothar?"

Lothar was moved by his friend's profound anguish; all three embraced in tearful reconciliation and swore everlasting love and friendship.

Nathanael felt as though a heavy burden had been lifted from him, as if, by resisting the dark power that had held him in thrall, he had saved his whole being from annihilation. He spent another three days with his dear friends and then went back to G——, where he had to remain for another year before returning home for good.

Not a word about Coppelius was said to Nathanael's mother; they all knew she could not think of him without horror, since, like Nathanael, she blamed him for her husband's death.

On returning to his lodgings Nathanael was astounded to find that the whole house had been burnt down, leaving nothing standing but the bare chimney shafts. The fire had broken out in the apothecary's laboratory on the ground floor and spread upwards; consequently there had been time for Nathanael's courageous and active friends to force their way into his room on the top floor and save his books, manuscripts, and instruments. They had transported everything undamaged to a room they had rented for him in another house, into which he at once moved. He did not pay any particular attention to the fact that he was now living opposite Professor Spallanzani; nor did he attach any special significance to the discovery that he could see out of his window straight into the room in which Olympia often sat alone, so that he could clearly distinguish her figure even though her features remained blurred. It did finally strike him that Olympia frequently sat for hours on end at a small table in the same position in which he had seen her when he looked through the glass door, doing nothing and staring across at him with an unwavering gaze. He had to admit that he had never seen a lovelier figure; at the same time, with Klara in his heart, he remained totally indifferent to the stiff and rigid Olympia, and only every now and then did he glance up from his textbook at the beautiful statue for a fleeting instant.

He was just writing to Klara when there was a soft knock at the door. It opened at his invitation and Coppola's repulsive face looked in. Nathanael quivered inwardly; but after what Spallanzani had told him about his countryman Coppola, and what he had solemnly promised his sweetheart regarding the Sandman Coppelius, he felt ashamed of his childish fear of ghosts, forcibly pulled himself together, and said as gently and calmly as he could : "I don't want a barometer, go away, please."

At this, however, Coppola came right into the room and exclaimed in a hoarse voice, his wide mouth twisted in a horrible laugh and his small eyes gleaming piercingly under their long, grey lashes : "All righta, no barometer! But I've gotta lovely eyes, lovely eyes!"

Horrified, Nathanael cried : "Eyes, you madman? How can you have eyes?"

Coppola instantly put away his barometers, thrust his hand into his capacious coat pockets, took out lorgnettes and spectacles and laid them down on the table. "See – see – spectacles to put ona your nose, those are my eyes, my lovely eyes!"

. So saying, he pulled out more and more spectacles, till the whole table began to glitter and sparkle. A myriad eyes glanced and winked and stared up at Nathanael; he could not look away from the table; Coppola laid down more and more spectacles, and the blood-red beams of their intersecting gaze flared in ever-wilder confusion and pierced Nathanael's breast. Overcome by uncontrollable horror, he seized Coppola's arm and cried out : "Stop, stop, you terrible man!"

Coppola, who had just been reaching into his pocket for

more spectacles, although the table was already covered, gently freed himself with the words: "Nothing there you lika? Well, here are fina glasses." So saying, he swept up the spectacles, put them back in his pocket, and drew a number of binoculars of all sizes from the side pocket of his coat. As soon as the spectacles had gone Nathanael became quite calm and, thinking of Klara, he could see that the terrifying spectre was solely the product of his own mind and that Coppola was a perfectly honest mechanic and optician and could not possibly be the double or ghost of the accursed Coppelius. Moreover, there was nothing out of the way about the binoculars which Coppola now put on the table, certainly nothing weird and ghostly as there had been about the spectacles. To make up for his previous behaviour, Nathanael decided to buy something. He picked up a small, very neatly made pair of pocket binoculars and looked out of the window to test them. Never in his life had he come across binoculars which brought objects so clear and close before his eyes. Involuntarily, he looked into Spallanzani's room; Olympia was sitting at the small table as usual, her arms resting on it and her hands folded.

Now, for the first time, Nathanael caught sight of Olympia's beautifully formed face. Only her eyes appeared to him curiously fixed and dead. But as he stared more and more intently through the glasses it seemed as though humid moonbeams were beginning to shine in Olympia's eyes. It was as though the power of sight were only now awaking, the flame of life flickering more and more brightly. Nathanael leaned out of the window as though bound to the spot by a spell, staring unceasingly at Olympia's heavenly beauty.

The sound of a throat being cleared woke him as though out of a deep sleep. Coppola was standing behind him. "*Tre zechini* – three ducats," he said. Nathanael, who had completely forgotten the optician, quickly paid him what he asked. "A fine pair of glasses, eh?" asked Coppola with his repulsive hoarse voice and malevolent laugh.

"Yes, yes," replied Nathanael irritably. "Goodbye, my friend."

Coppola left the room, but not without casting many strange sidelong glances at Nathanael. He heard the optician laughing loudly as he went down the stairs. "Aha," thought Nathanael, "I suppose he is laughing at me because I paid too dearly for the binoculars – I paid too dearly!" As he muttered these words softly to himself, he seemed to hear a deep sigh, like a dying man's, echo terrifyingly round the room, and fear stopped his breath. But it was he himself who had sighed, he realized that. "Klara is quite right to consider me a preposterous ghost-seer," he told himself; "it is stupid, more than stupid to be so strangely frightened by the foolish thought that I paid too dearly for Coppola's binoculars; I can see absolutely no reason for it."

Then he sat down to finsh his letter to Klara; but a glance out of the window showed him that Olympia was still sitting where she had been, and instantly, as though impelled by an irresistible force, he jumped up, seized Coppola's glasses, and could not tear himself away from the seductive vision of Olympia until his friend Siegmund called him to Professor Spallanzani's lecture. The curtain was pulled right across the fateful door and he could catch no glimpse of Olympia. Nor did he see her during the next two days, although he hardly left his window and kept on looking across through Coppola's binoculars. On the third day her window was actually covered with a curtain. In utter despair and driven by longing and hot desire, he hurried out beyond the city gates. Olympia's figure floated before him in the air, emerged from the undergrowth, and stared at him with big, shining eyes out of the sparkling stream. Klara's image had completely faded from his mind; he thought of nothing but Olympia and lamented in a loud and tearful voice : "O my lofty, noble star of love, did you rise only to vanish again and leave me in a gloomy, hopeless darkness?"

On his return home, he became aware of a great deal of noise and activity in Spallanzani's house. The doors were open, all sorts of gear was being carried in, the first-floor windows had been taken off their hinges, maids were busily sweeping and dusting, running to and fro with big hairbrooms, while inside the house carpenters and upholsterers were banging and hammering. Nathanael stood stock still in the street with amazement. Siegmund came up to him and asked with a laugh: "Well, what do you say about old Spallanzani?" Nathanael replied that he couldn't say anything, because he knew absolutely nothing about the Professor; on the contrary, he observed to his astonishment that the silent, gloomy house had become the scene of feverish activity. Siegmund told him that tomorrow Spallanzani was giving a big party, concert, and ball, to which half the university was invited. Rumour had it that Spallanzani was going to show his daughter in public for the first time, after for so long anxiously concealing her from human eyes.

Nathanael received an invitation card and went to the Professor's house at the appointed hour, when carriages were already driving up and lights shining in the decorated rooms. The gathering was large and brilliant. Olympia made her appearance very richly and tastefully dressed. Everyone admired her beautifully modelled face and figure. Her rather strange hollow back and wasp waist seemed the result of excessively tight clothing. There was something measured and stiff about her gait and posture that struck many people as unpleasant, but it was attributed to a feeling of constraint due to the social occasion. The concert began. Olympia played the harpsichord with great proficiency and also sang a *bravura aria* in a high-pitched, almost shrill, bell-like voice. Nathanael was quite enchanted; he was standing in the back row and could not fully distinguish

Olympia's features in the dazzling candlelight. Surreptitiously, therefore, he pulled out Coppola's binoculars and looked at her.

He discovered to his astonishment that she was gazing at him full of longing, that every note she sang was reflected in the amorous glances which pierced and set fire to his heart. Her skilful roulades seemed to Nathanael the heavenly exultations of a spirit transfigured by love, and when finally the *cadenza* of the long trill echoed shrilly through the room, he felt as though he were being clasped by her hot arms and, unable to restrain his anguish and delight, he shouted loudly : "Olympia." Everyone looked round at him and many laughed. The organist from the cathedral merely pulled an even sourer face than before, however, and said : "Now, now !" The concert was at an end, the ball began.

"Now to dance – with her !" This was Nathanael's one wish and purpose; but how was he to find the courage to ask the queen of the festivities to dance with him? And yet, after the dance had started, he found himself to his own surprise standing close by Olympia, who had not yet been asked to dance. Barely able to stammer a few words, he seized her hand. It was like ice; a cold shudder passed through him; he gazed into Olympia's eyes, which beamed back at him full of love and longing; and at the same instant a pulse seemed to start beating in the cold hand and the warm life-blood started flowing. Simultaneously the fires of love in Nathanael's breast began to burn more brightly; he put his arm round the lovely Olympia and whirled with her through the lines of dancers.

He imagined that he had been dancing in very good time to the music, but he soon observed from the peculiar, fixed rhythm in which Olympia danced, and which often confused him, that he was badly out of step. Nevertheless, he did not want to dance with any other woman and would have felt like murdering anyone else who asked Olympia to dance. To his astonishment this happened only twice, however;

thereafter Olympia was left sitting at every dance and he partnered her again and again. Had Nathanael had eyes for anything but the lovely Olympia, any number of unpleasant quarrels would have been inevitable; for the half-suppressed laughter that broke out in this corner or in that among the young men was obviously directed towards the lovely Olympia, whom for some unknown reason the students continually watched.

Heated by the dancing and the plentiful wine he had drunk, Nathanael had cast aside all his usual shyness. He sat beside Olympia, her hand in his, and spoke with burning fervour of his love in words that no one understood, neither he nor Olympia. But perhaps the latter did, for she gazed steadfastly into his eyes and sighed time after time : "Oh – oh – oh !" Whereupon Nathanael exclaimed : "O magnificent, heavenly woman – ray shining from love's land of promise beyond this earthly realm – deep soul in which my whole being is mirrored," and more of the same kind; but Olympia merely went on sighing : "Oh, oh !"

Professor Spallanzani walked past the happy couple and gave them a curiously satisfied smile. It seemed to Nathanael that, although he himself was in a totally different and higher world, it was getting noticeably dark down here in Professor Spallanzani's house; he looked round and saw with no little dismay that the last two lights in the room were burning low and on the point of going out. Music and dancing had long since come to an end. "We must part, we must part," he shouted in wild despair; he kissed Olympia's hand, then he bent down to her mouth; ice-cold lips met his burning hot ones ! Just as when he touched Olympia's cold hand, he felt a shudder run through him; the legend of the dead bride flashed across his mind; but Olympia had pressed him to her, and in the kiss her lips seemed to warm to life.

Professor Spallanzani walked slowly through the empty room; his steps echoed hollowly and his figure looked sinister and ghostly as the shadows cast by the guttering candles played over it.

"Do you love me? Do you love me, Olympia? Just say one word! Do you love me?" Nathanael whispered, but all Olympia sighed as she stood up was, "Oh, oh, oh!"

"My lovely, splendid star of love," said Nathanael, "now that you have appeared to me you will illumine my soul for evermore!"

"Oh, oh!" replied Olympia as she strode away.

Nathanael followed her; they came to a stop in front of the Professor. "You had an extraordinarily animated conversation with my daughter," said the latter with a smile. "If you like talking to the stupid girl, my dear Nathanael, you are welcome to visit us at any time."

Nathanael left with all heaven ablaze in his breast. Spallanzani's party was the talk of the town for the next few days. Despite the fact that the Professor had done everything to create an impression of magnificence, wits found plenty of *gaucheries* and oddities to comment upon. A particular target of criticism was the rigid, mute, Olympia, who, notwithstanding her beautiful outward appearance, was credited with total idiocy, which was assumed to be the reason why Spallanzani had kept her hidden for so long. Nathanael felt inwardly enraged as he listened to all this, but he said nothing. "What would be the use of pointing out to these fellows that it is their own idiocy that prevents them from recognizing Olympia's profound and splendid mind?" he thought to himself.

"Will you please tell me, friend," Siegmund said to him one day, "how an intelligent fellow like you can possibly have fallen for that waxen-faced wooden doll across the road?"

Nathanael was about to fly into a rage, but he quickly gained control of himself and answered: "Tell me, Siegmund, how Olympia's heavenly charms have escaped your eye, normally so quick to discern beauty, and your alert mind? And yet on that account, thanks be to fate, I do not have you as a rival; for if we were rivals one of us would die a violent death."

Siegmund saw how things stood with his friend, adroitly gave way, and after stating that there was never any point in arguing about the object of a person's love, added : "But it is strange that many of us are of very much the same opinion about Olympia. She seems to us – forgive me for saying so, friend – curiously stiff and inert. Her figure is symmetrical and so is her face, that's true. She might be considered beautiful, if her eyes were not so completely devoid of life, I would almost say of vision. Her walk is strangely measured, every movement seems to be controlled by clockwork. She plays and sings with the unpleasantly accurate but lifeless rhythm of a singing machine, and her dancing is the same. We found Olympia thoroughly uncanny, we didn't want to have anything to do with her, we felt she was only acting the part of a living being and that there was something odd about her."

Nathanael did not yield to the feeling of bitterness that assailed him as he listened to Siegmund's words; mastering his resentment, he merely said very gravely : "Olympia may well appear uncanny to you cold, prosaic people. A poetic nature is accessible only to the poet. Her loving gaze reached me alone and irradiated by thoughts and feelings; only in Olympia's love do I find myself. You may not like the fact that she does not chatter away and make dull conversation like most shallow-minded people. She utters few words, it's true; but those few words are true hieroglyphs that express the inner world filled with love and higher knowledge of the spiritual life as seen from the viewpoint of the world beyond. But you have no understanding for all this and I am wasting my words."

"May God preserve you, friend," said Siegmund very gently, almost sadly. "It seems to me that you are on an evil path. You can rely on me if everything – no, I will say no more!"

Nathanael suddenly had the feeling that the cold, prosaic Siegmund meant very well by him; he therefore shook the proffered hand with great warmth.

Nathanael had totally forgotten that there was in the world a girl called Klara, whom he used to love. His mother ... Lothar ... they had all vanished from his memory; he lived only for Olympia, with whom he sat for hours on end every day talking wildly of love, sympathy, and the affinity of souls, to all of which Olympia listened with great reverence. From the depths of his desk, Nathanael dug up everything he had ever written. There were poems, fantasies, novels, stories, and the number was increasing daily by a multitude of high-flown sonnets, stanzas, canzonets. All this he read to Olympia for hours at a time without tiring. Never had he found such a wonderful listener. She didn't embroider or knit, she didn't stare out of the window, she didn't play with a lap-dog or cat, she didn't twist scraps of paper or anything else between her fingers, she had no need to force a cough to cover up a yawn; she gazed steadfastly into her lover's eyes for hours on end without moving, and her own eyes became continually more ardent, more alive. Only when Nathanael stood up and kissed her hand and her lips, did she murmur, "Oh, oh!" and then, "Good night, dearest!"

"O glorious, profound soul," cried Nathanael when he was back in his room, "you, and you alone, understand me utterly." He trembled with inward delight when he thought of the wonderful harmony that was growing daily between his mind and Olympia's; it seemed to him that Olympia had spoken about his works, about his whole poetic talent, from the depths of his own soul, as though the voice had come from within himself. This must indeed have been the case, for Olympia never uttered a word more than those already recorded, but even at moments of lucidity, for example on first waking up in the morning, when Nathanael became aware of Olympia's passivity and taciturnity, he said to himself : "What are mere words? A single look from her heavenly eyes expresses more than any earthly language. Can a child of heaven confine herself within the narrow circle drawn by wretched earthly needs?"

Professor Spallanzani seemed highly delighted over his daughter's relations with Nathanael, giving the latter all sorts of unequivocal signs of his benevolence; and when Nathanael ventured to drop a few oblique hints about a possible union with his daughter, the Professor smiled all over his face and commented that he would leave his daughter a completely free choice.

Encouraged by these words, and with burning desire in his heart, Nathanael resolved to beseech Olympia the very next day to put clearly into words what her loving glances had long since told him : that she wished to be his for evermore. He looked for the ring his mother had given him when he left, intending to bestow it upon Olympia as a symbol of his devotion and of the new life upon which they were about to embark together. As he looked he came across the letters from Klara and Lothar; he cast them indifferently aside, found the ring, put it in his pocket, and hurried across to Olympia.

While still on the stairs and landing he heard an extraordinary hubbub that seemed to be coming from Spallanzani's study : stamping, clattering, thudding, banging on the door, interspersed with curses and imprecations. "Let go, let go, you rogue, you villain! ... Did I give everything I had for that? ... Ha ha ha ha, that wasn't our wager. ... I made the eyes. ... And I the clockwork. ... To hell with you and your wretched clockwork, you paltry mechanic! ... Satan. ... Stop. ... Miserable wise-twister. ... Fiendish beast! ... Stop. ... Get out. ... Let go!" The voices that thus raved in indistinguishable confusion were those of Spallanzani and the abominable Coppelius.

Nathanael rushed in, seized by a nameless fear. The Professor was holding a female figure by the shoulders, Coppola the Italian had her by the feet, and they were twisting and tugging her this way and that, fighting for her with unbridled rage. Nathanael recoiled in horror when he recognized the figure as Olympia. Bursting with fury, he was about to tear his beloved away from the frantic pair when Coppola, twisting the figure with a giant's strength, wrenched it from the Professor's hands and struck him such a blow with it that he toppled backwards over the table – on which stood phials, retorts, bottles, and glass cylinders – staggered and fell; all the vessels crashed to the ground in fragments. Then Coppola threw the figure over his shoulder and ran down the stairs with a terrible, screeching laugh, the figure's dangling feet bumping and rapping woodenly on the stairs as he ran.

Nathanael stood transfixed – he had seen all too clearly that Olympia's deathly pale waxen face had no eyes, but only black cavities : she was a lifeless doll. Spallanzani was writhing on the floor; his head, chest, and arm had been cut by broken glass, and the blood was pouring out like water from a spring. But he summoned his strength and cried : "After him, after him, what are you waiting for? Coppelius has stolen my best automaton. I worked on it for twenty years, I put everything into it. The mechanism, the walk, the power of speech are mine; the eyes he stole from you. The villain, the rogue, after him, bring back my Olympia. There are your eyes!"

Now Nathanael saw a pair of blood-flecked eyes staring up at him from the floor; Spallanzani seized them in his uninjured hand and flung them at his breast. Then madness gripped him with red-hot claws and entered into him, disrupting his mind and senses. "Hoa – hoa – hoa! Circle of flames, circle of flames, spin circle of flames – merrily – merrily! Wooden doll – hoa – spin, wooden doll. . . ." With these words he hurled himself upon the Professor and squeezed his throat. He would have throttled him, but the din had attracted a number of people, who forced their way in and pulled off the frenzied Nathanael, thus saving the life of the Professor, whose wounds were then bandaged. Strong as he was, Siegmund was unable to hold his raging friend, who kept screaming, "Wooden doll, spin," at the top of his voice and striking about him with his fists. He was finally overcome by the united efforts of several men, who threw him to the ground and tied him up. His words degenerated into a hideous animal bellowing. Frenziedly struggling, he was taken away to the madhouse.

Before continuing my account of what happened to the unfortunate Nathanael I should like to assure any reader who may feel some sympathy with the skilful mechanic and automata-maker Spallanzani that he completely recovered from his wounds. He had to leave the university, however, because Nathanael's story had attracted a great deal of attention, and people considered it unpardonable deceit to have smuggled a wooden doll into well-conducted tea parties (which Olympia had, in fact, successfully attended) in the guise of a living person. Jurists called it a fraudulent imposture and considered it worthy of all the more severe punishment because it was directed against the public and undetected by anyone (apart from a few highly intelligent students) – although everyone, wise after the event, now pointed to all sorts of facts which they claimed had struck them as suspicious. There was very little sense in these claims, however. Why, for example, should anyone's suspicions have been aroused by the fact that, according to an elegant gentleman given to attending tea parties, Olympia had contradicted the normal custom by sneezing more often than she yawned? This gentleman claimed that the sneezing automatically wound up Olympia's hidden mechanism, which had audibly creaked as she sneezed, and so on. The professor of poetry and rhetoric took a pinch of snuff, snapped his snuff-box shut, cleared his throat, and solemnly declared : "Ladies and gentlemen, do you not see the point of it all? The whole thing is an allegory – an extended metaphor! You understand what I mean! *Sapienti sat!*"

But many gentlemen were not reassured; the story of the automaton had made a deep impression, and a horrible distrust of human figures insinuated itself into people's minds. To make sure they were not in love with a wooden doll, many lovers insisted upon their mistresses singing and dancing out of time, embroidering, knitting, or playing with a lap-dog while being read to, and, above all, not merely listening but also speaking from time to time in such a way as to prove that they really thought and felt. Many lovers became more firmly and joyfully allied than ever, but others gradually drifted apart. "You really can't be sure," commented a few. At tea parties people yawned with tremendous frequency and never sneezed, to avert all possible suspicion.

Spallanzani, as I have said, had to leave the city to escape criminal proceedings for fraudulently introducing an automaton into human society. Coppola had also disappeared.

Nathanael awoke as though out of a frightful dream, opened his eyes, and felt an indescribable bliss permeate him with a gentle, heavenly warmth. He was lying on the bed in his room at home; Klara was bending over him, and his mother and Lothar were standing close by.

"At last, at last, my dearly beloved Nathanael. Now you are cured of your terrible illness, now you are mine again!" cried Klara from the depths of her heart, taking Nathanael into her arms.

Bright, hot tears of longing and delight welled from his eyes, and he groaned : "Klara, my Klara!"

Siegmund, who had stood loyally by his friend in his hour of need, came in. Nathanael held out his hand to him, saying : "Faithful friend, you did not forsake me."

All trace of madness had vanished, and Nathanael soon

35

regained his strength in the loving care of his mother, sweet-heart, and friends. Good fortune had meanwhile entered the house; a miserly old uncle, of whom no one had had any hopes, had died and left Nathanael's mother not merely a tidy fortune but also a small farm in a pleasant district not far from the town. Nathanael, his mother, Klara, whom he now intended to marry, and Lothar planned to move into the farm. Nathanael had grown gentler and more childlike than ever before, and now fully appreciated the heavenly purity of Klara's noble spirit. Only as Siegmund was saying goodbye to him did he remark : "By God, friend, I was on an evil road, but an angel led me to the path of sanity in time! It was Klara! . . ." Siegmund would let him say no more for fear that deeply wounding memories might return to him too vividly.

The time came for the four happy people to move into the little farm. They were walking at midday through the streets of the town, where they had made a number of purchases. The high tower of the Town Hall cast its gigantic shadow over the market-place. "Oh, let us climb it once more and look across at the distant mountains," suggested Klara. No sooner said than done. Nathanael and Klara ascended the tower; Nathanael's mother went home with the servant; while Lothar, feeling disinclined to mount so many steps, stayed down below. The two lovers were standing arm in arm on the topmost gallery of the tower, looking down into the fragrant woods beyond which the blue mountains rose like a giant city.

"Just look at that strange little grey bush that really seems to be striding out towards us," exclaimed Klara. Nathanael automatically put his hand in his side pocket, found Coppola's binoculars, and looked slightly to one side. Klara was standing in the way of the glasses. There was a convulsive twitching in his pulse and arteries. He stared at Klara, his face deathly pale; but soon streams of fire glowed and spurted from his eyes, he began to roar horribly like a hunted beast; then he bounded into the air and, interspersing his words with ghastly laughter, yelled : "Wooden doll, spin! Wooden doll, spin!" He seized Klara with tremendous force and tried to hurl her down from the tower; but Klara, with the strength of desperation, clung to the parapet. Lothar heard the madman raving, he heard Klara's cry of terror; a terrible foreboding took possession of him, he raced up the stairs; the door to the second flight was shut. Klara's cries of distress were growing louder. Frantic with rage and fear, Lothar hurled himself against the door, which finally gave way. Klara's cries were now becoming fainter and fainter. "Help – save me – save me. . . ." Her voice died away. "She is dead, murdered by the madman," cried Lothar. The door to the gallery was also shut. Despair gave him the strength of a giant; he burst the door from its hinges. Merciful God – Klara, in the grip of the raving Nathanael, was hanging from the gallery in mid-air; only one hand still clung to the iron railing. Quick as lightning, Lothar seized his sister, pulled her back and smashed his fist into the face of the madman, who stumbled backwards and let go of his prey.

Lothar raced down the stairs with his unconscious sister in his arms. She was saved. Nathanael was now rampaging round the gallery, bounding into the air and shouting : "Circle of flames, spin – circle of flames, spin!" Attracted by his yelling, a crowd gathered; in the midst of it was the gigantic figure of the lawyer Coppelius, who had just arrived in the town and had come straight to the market-place. People wanted to go up and overpower the madman. Coppelius laughed and said : "Just wait, he'll come down of his own accord." Then he stared aloft with the rest. Nathanael suddenly stopped in his tracks, leaned forward, caught sight of Coppelius and with an ear-splitting shriek of "Ha, lovely eyes, lovely eyes," leapt over the parapet.

By the time Nathanael lay on the pavement with his skull smashed, Coppelius had vanished.

Many years later, Klara was reported to have been seen in a place far from her home town, sitting hand-in-hand with a friendly looking man outside the door of a beautiful country house, with two merry little boys playing in front of her. From this we may infer that Klara eventually found the calm domestic bliss which her serene and cheerful nature demanded and which Nathanael with his perpetual inner strife could never have given her.

CPSIA information can be obtained at www.ICGtesting.com
Printed in the USA
BVOW08s1728030314

346526BV00001B/147/P